"We are ready!" said Scout Brother. "We're ready to ride the rapids."

The Bear Scouts were going to paddle their canoe down the Rapid River. They were trying to earn the White Water Merit Badge.

They launched their canoe and climbed aboard.

"Just a minute!"
called a voice.
It was Too-Tall
Grizzly and his gang.
They had a boat, too.
"How about a race?"
said Too-Tall. "Let's have
a race down the river."

The Berenstain
BEAR SCOUTS
AND THE
WHITE WATER
MYSTERY

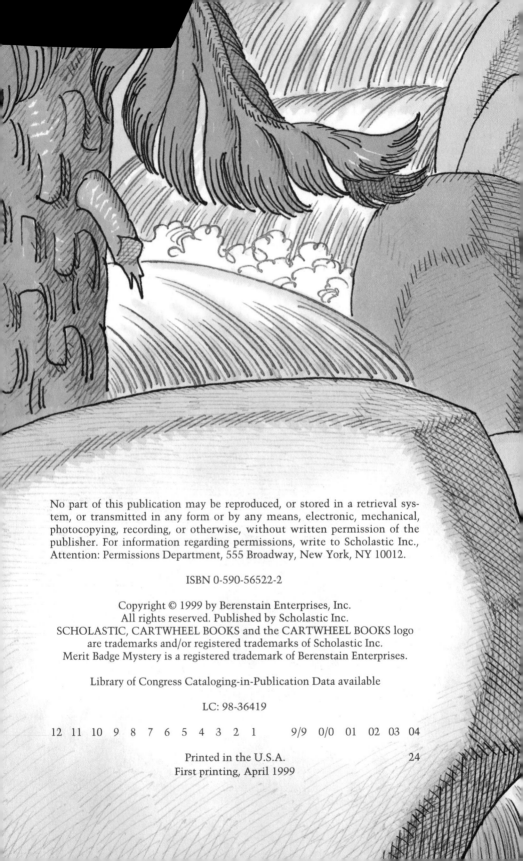

ISBN 0-590-56522-2

Copyright © 1999 by Berenstain Enterprises, Inc.
All rights reserved. Published by Scholastic Inc.
SCHOLASTIC, CARTWHEEL BOOKS and the CARTWHEEL BOOKS logo
are trademarks and/or registered trademarks of Scholastic Inc.
Merit Badge Mystery is a registered trademark of Berenstain Enterprises.

Library of Congress Cataloging-in-Publication Data available

LC: 98-36419

12 11 10 9 8 7 6 5 4 3 2 1   9/9 0/0 01 02 03 04

Printed in the U.S.A.   24
First printing, April 1999

The Berenstain BEAR SCOUTS

AND THE

WHITE WATER MYSTERY

Stan & Jan Berenstain

Illustrated by Michael Berenstain

Cartwheel
·B·O·O·K·S·®
SCHOLASTIC INC.
New York   Toronto   London   Auckland   Sydney

"We're working on our White Water
Merit Badge, Too-Tall," explained Scout Sister.

"What's the matter?" asked Too-Tall.
"Scared?"

"Okay, wise guy," said Brother. "We'll have
a race. How far?"

"Down the rapids, around the bend to the
old oak tree," said Too-Tall.

"And may the best cubs win," added Smirk.

The Bear Scouts and the Too-Tall gang pushed their canoes out into the river.

"Ready," said Scout Fred, "get set, PADDLE!"

They all began to paddle as fast as they could.

At first, the two boats were neck and neck. Then, the Bear Scouts began to pull ahead. They were better paddlers than the Too-Tall gang.

The Bear Scouts all paddled together.
"Stroke! Stroke! Stroke!" Brother
called to keep the time.
The Too-Tall gang paddled every
which way.

"Look out!" warned Scout Lizzy.
"We're coming to the rapids."
White water boiled up ahead of them.

"Stroke! Stroke! Uh-oh!" said Scout Brother as they shot down into the rapids. They swept past Big Bear Rock.

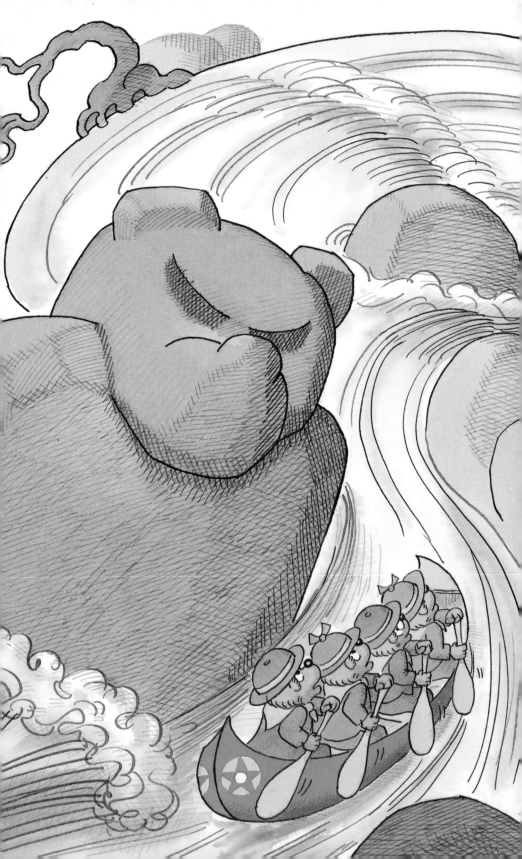

They curved around
Swirling Whirlpool.
They bumped down
Twenty Step Falls.

When they reached the bottom of the falls
they looked back. The Too-Tall gang were
nowhere to be seen.

"I guess they chickened out when they
saw those rapids," said Scout Fred.

"Hurray!" shouted the Bear Scouts.
"We're going to win!" They crossed their
paddles. "Motto time!" they cried. "One
for all and all for one!"

But as they drifted around the bend in the river, they saw an amazing sight.

There, tied to the old oak tree that marked the finish line, was a boat.

And there, leaning against the tree, was — the Too-Tall gang!

The Bear Scouts' mouths hung open.
"How?" they gasped. "How did you
get ahead of us?"

"Nothin' to it!" said Too-Tall with a grin.
"We just paddled around one side of Big Bear
Rock while you paddled around the other
side."

"Yeah!" smirked Smirk. "You were so
busy with your 'Stroke! Stroke! Stroke!' that
you never noticed us."

The Too-Tall gang began to dance around the Bear Scouts, pretending to paddle.

"Stroke! Stroke! Stroke!" they chanted.

STROKE! STROKE! STROKE!

The Bear Scouts were furious. They knew
that they had really won the race. They
knew that they had been cheated, somehow.
But, *how?*

It was a mystery.
The white water mystery!

That's when Lizzy noticed Dr. Wise Old Owl sitting in the branches of the old oak tree. Maybe he could explain.

"Dr. Wise Old Owl! Dr. Wise Old Owl!" called Lizzy. "Can you tell us how Too-Tall won the race?"

Dr. Wise Old Owl turned
his head all the way around,
blinked, and said:

One boat at the start,
Then round the bend,
There's a path to boat two
At the other end.

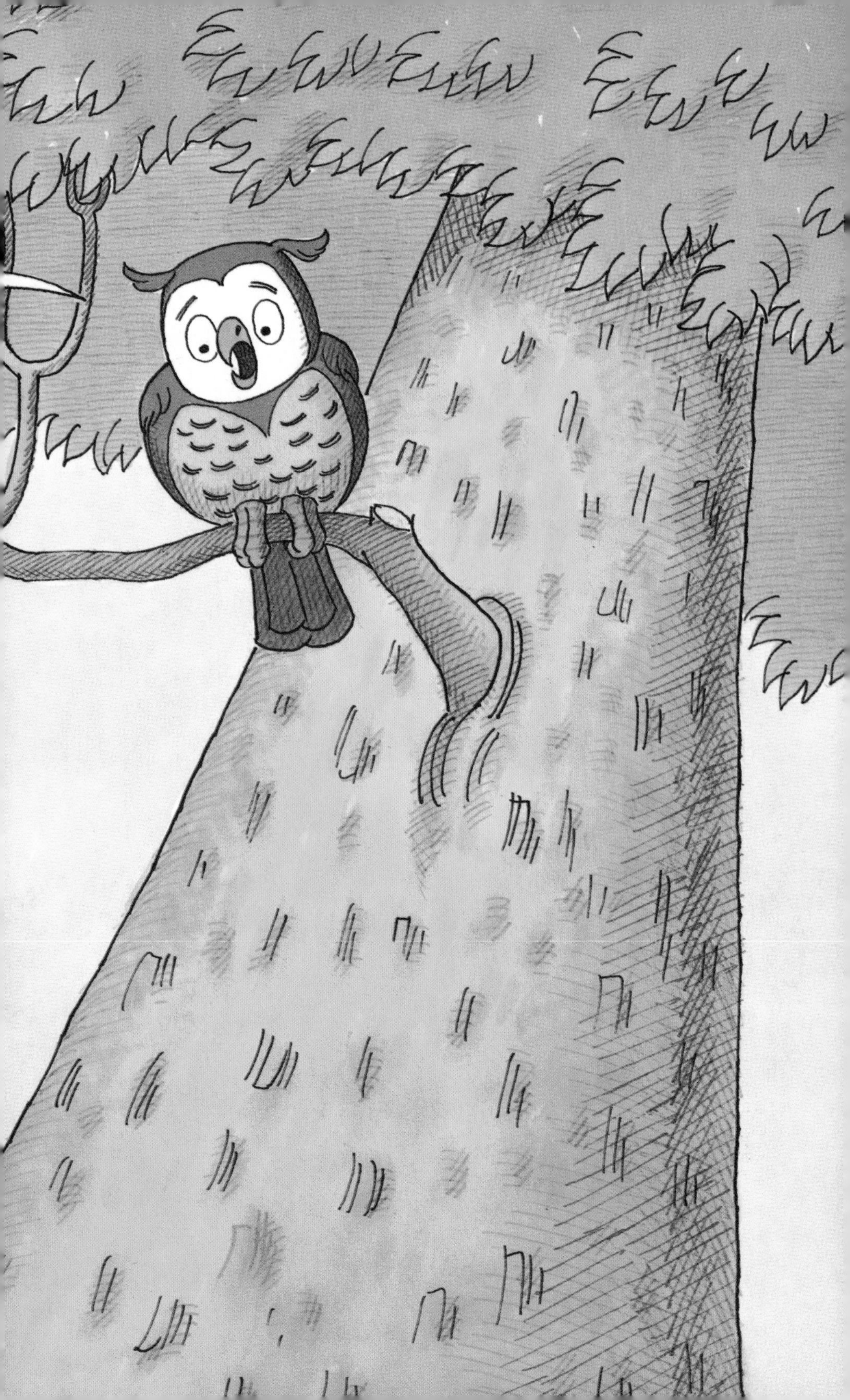

"A path?" wondered Fred. "Where?"

"There!" said Sister, pointing. A path led into the woods. "Let's follow it and see where it leads."

The Bear Scouts followed the path through the woods back to the riverbank around the bend.

"Look!" cried Lizzy. "There's another boat tied up at the other end."

"One boat at the start...," said Brother, rubbing his chin. "This must be the boat that Too-Tall used at the start of the race."

"And while we were shooting the rapids," Sister went on, "they hopped out, ran along the path to boat two at the other end..."

"And pretended to win the race!" added Fred.

The Bear Scouts ran back along the path.

"Hey!" they yelled at the Too-Tall gang.
"You didn't win the race! We did! You cheated!"

Too-Tall just shrugged.

"We have a motto, too," he told them. "If you can't beat 'em, cheat 'em."

The Bear Scouts not only won the race, they earned their White Water Merit Badge as well. They hung it on their clubhouse wall with their other badges.

The Too-Tall gang had to make their own badge to hang on their clubhouse wall. It was the "If You Can't Beat 'Em, Cheat 'Em" *D*emerit Badge!